GEORGE The Generous Giraffe

By: Kam Trumbo

Illustrated By: Fanny Liem

First Printing: May 2015
Second Edition: November 2016

For information on upcoming books by Kameron Trumbo, visit TrumboBooks.com

ISBN-10: 0996170308
ISBN-13: 978-0996170307

Special Thanks:

I'm very thankful to everyone who helped fund this book. I appreciate each person who provided support & encouragement.

A special thanks to Adrian Trumbo, Semion Bolotin, Chuck Wang, and Connie & Dave Erickson for your generosity in helping make this dream of creating this book a reality for me and my family!

In this world of animals both big and small-
There is one unique animal who stands very tall.

His name is George the generous giraffe.
He makes his friends giggle and laugh.

Because George loves
to give his things away.

George gives away clothes, toys, and things he does not need.

He donates his
time and skills-
even his money, indeed!

Last week George helped
Mr. Kangaroo cut his grass.

On Wednesdays he reads to Mrs. Peacock's class.

George tells a joke when he gives something away. His humor and generosity brightens everyone's day!

One day George looked around,
and he had given everything he had.

Now how would he
help those in need?

He felt so sad.

With no extra toys, clothes, or money left to give out,

George had to think of another way - not just sit and pout.

Late that night while lying in bed,
George had an idea pop into his head.

George thought of a way to earn money by making others laugh out loud.

By being creative, he would have more to give and would feel so proud.

George and his friends would use
their talents to put on a show.

They would sell tickets and invite everyone they know!

The day finally arrived, and George's talent show began!
Animals came to enjoy the show from all across the land.

His friend Bo the Beaver sang a song and played the guitar,

and Ally the Alligator sold treats at the snack bar.

George told funny jokes and made everyone laugh.

This made him a super happy and thankful giraffe.

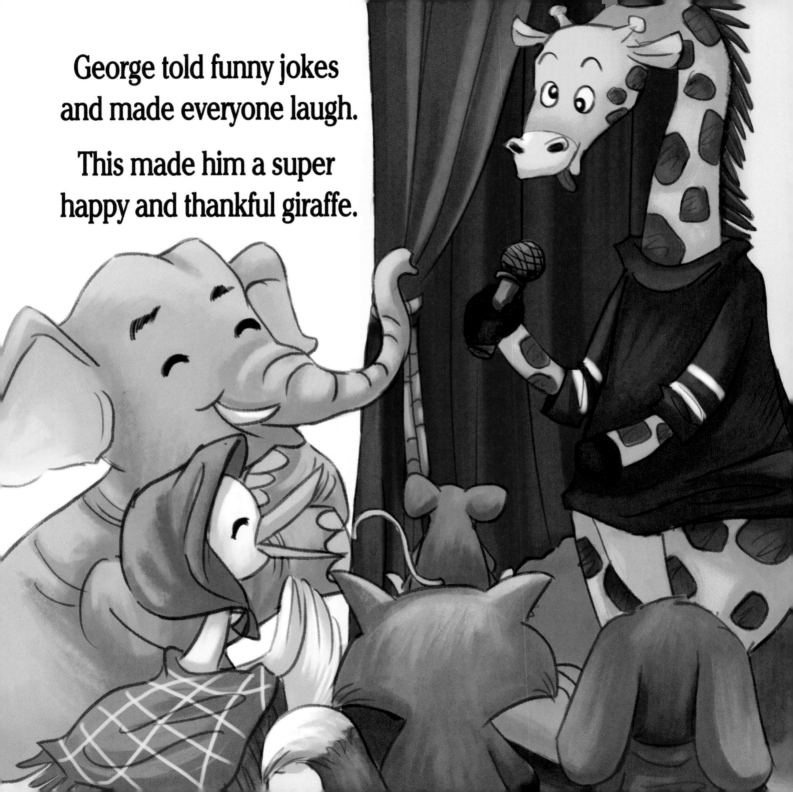

The show was a hit and the fans yelled, "bravo!" out loud.

George, Bo, and Ally smiled and then bowed.

They all chose to continue with their generous ways, donating their time, skills, and money for the rest of their days.

You see George has learned,
and hopes you will believe. . .
when you give and are
generous, you actually receive.

About The Author:

Kameron Trumbo lives in Oregon with his family and pets.

He loves to snowboard, sing (out of tune), ride his mountain bike, and travel.

Learn more about Kameron and the other books he's written at TrumboBooks.com